THE STICKY WITCH

HILARY McKAY

With illustrations by

Mike Phillips

Barrington Stoke

For Helena Cochrane,
with love from Bella and Hilary McKay

First published in 2016 in Great Britain by
Barrington Stoke Ltd
18 Walker Street, Edinburgh, EH3 7LP

www.barringtonstoke.co.uk

4u2read edition based on *The Sticky Witch*
(Barrington Stoke, 2010)

A CIP catalogue record for this book is available from the British Library upon request

ISBN: 978-1-78112-599-1

Printed in China by Leo

Contents

Chapter 1
The Raft

Tom, Ellie and Whiskers the Cat stood at the edge of the sea.

Tom made up his mind to be brave.

Ellie made up her mind not to fuss.

Whiskers made up her mind to stay safe on dry land for ever and ever. She didn't like the look of the mad, tatty raft that was rocking to and fro out on the choppy green water.

Tom and Ellie's mum and dad had made the raft out of junk. The sort of junk that gets washed up on a beach. Plastic bottles and old tyres and parts of a van that had fallen off a cliff.

Tom and Ellie's parents were off to sail around the world in their raft of rubbish. "The raft will show everyone the rubbish that's been thrown into the sea. We're helping to save the planet," they said. "Also it will be great fun."

Tom and Ellie didn't think it would be great fun. But they thought it would be better to sail round the world on a home-made raft than stay behind with terrible Aunt Tab. Only no one gave them a choice.

"Children have to go to school," their parents said. "It's the law."

'School's OK,' Tom and Ellie thought. 'We don't mind school. It's Aunt Tab we mind.'

But Tom and Ellie had made up their minds to be brave and not fuss. So they waved at their mum and dad out on the sea and tried to look happy.

"Goodbye!" their parents shouted as they sailed away. "See you soon! Three years will go in a flash! Clean your teeth every morning! Do your homework every night! And write as often as you can!"

And then they were gone.

Tom and Ellie stopped waving and smiling, and stared out to sea.

As far as they could see there was nothing but sky and sun and wild green water.

"Sunk," Ellie said.

"No," said Tom.

"What then?" Ellie asked.

"Just gone, between one wave and another."

Ellie picked up Whiskers and hid her face in her soft, gold fur.

Neither of them said anything after that, but at last they grew tired and they turned back to the village. As they walked, Ellie thought how useful it would be to have wings, or a life-boat, or normal parents. And Tom thought that three years was a very long time indeed.

No cheerful thoughts came to either of them until they reached the village shop.

It had a rack of postcards outside.

"They said 'write'!" Tom said. "'As often as you can!' Help me choose a postcard! Come on! Here's some cat ones. Do any of them look like Whiskers? What about this?"

"Too orange," Ellie said.

Tom picked out another card. "This then?"

"The cat in that picture doesn't have white paws," said Ellie. "Perhaps this one?" She picked up a postcard of a golden tabby cat with stripes like a tiger and snow white paws.

"Wrong colour eyes," said Tom. "Not green enough. Never mind. It'll do. Come on, let's buy it."

On the card they wrote –

Dear Parents, if you have not sunk.

The news is that we hope very much that you haven't sunk.

With love from Ellie and Tom and Whiskers the Cat.

and they wrote this address:

The Raft on its Way Round the World
If it has not sunk
The Sea

Then they put the card into an empty lemonade bottle, ran back to the beach and threw it out to sea. This all made Tom and Ellie feel much better.

But then they went home to Aunt Tab's, and that made them feel much worse.

Chapter 2
Aunt Tab

Aunt Tab was not Tom and Ellie's real aunt. Aunt Tab was a person who had answered an advert from Tom and Ellie's parents. This is what the advert had said –

WANTED

Extra special and kind person to look after two wonderful children

And Whiskers the Cat

All expenses paid ... In cash

A lot of people said they were happy to take care of Whiskers the Cat, and a few said they'd look after one wonderful child.

One or two offered to have two wonderful children.

But only Aunt Tab had said she would have two wonderful children and Whiskers the Cat.

And so Tom and Ellie's parents chose Aunt Tab to look after Tom and Ellie while they sailed around the world. Tom and Ellie had to move to her house and start at a new school, with new friends and new teachers.

Tom and Ellie and Whiskers had met Aunt Tab for the first time that morning. She had looked at them and said in a very grumpy way, "You don't look wonderful to me!"

Aunt Tab's cottage was the last one in the village. She was waiting for them at the door as they came up the street.

"Well, well, so the goodbyes are over!" she said. "And the raft sank, I hear! Dear, dear, never mind! As a matter of fact, I thought it might. Now, here are The Rules. A copy for each of you to carry about and two for your bedroom walls. I have also put one in the bathroom, and one in the kitchen.

The Rules were –

No Fluff
No Crying
No Silly Questions
NO PLAYING IN THE PRIVATE POND

"That cat," Aunt Tab said, "has broken Rule Number 1 already! It is all fluff! Must you keep her?"

"Of course we must!" Ellie cried. "Tom! Tom! Tell her we must keep Whiskers!"

"No crying!" Aunt Tab snapped. "Rule Number 2!"

Rules
1. No fluff.
2. No crying.
3. No silly questions.
4.
NO PLAYING IN THE PRIVATE POND!

Tom was very brave. “Of course we must keep Whiskers!” he said.

“Pity,” Aunt Tab said. “I don’t like fluff. And I detest whiskers.”

“What’s wrong with Whiskers?”

“No silly questions,” Aunt Tab said. “Rule Number 3! Stand still, little girl! There!”

Aunt Tab took out some huge scissors. *Snip!* they went. *Snip!*

And in seconds the messy orange plaits that had stuck out from Ellie’s head were gone.

“PUT THEM BACK!” Ellie yelled.

“Don’t be silly, dear,” said Aunt Tab. “Now – your brother!”

“What?”

Tom’s ginger spikes flew into the air.

Snip! Snip! Snip!

"There!"

Tom and Ellie grabbed their heads and stared. At each other. At Aunt Tab. At clever Whiskers, who had jumped up onto a high shelf.

"I'll sort the cat out later," Aunt Tab said. "Put a hat on if you get chilly! Now, dears, bed!"

"What, no supper?" Ellie asked.

"I thought you'd be much too upset to eat supper," Aunt Tab said in a very surprised voice. "Supper, after your parents sank before your eyes! What very hard hearts you have!"

Still, she did make supper. Treacle sandwiches on sticky plates, and milk in sticky glasses. Tom and Ellie soon found that everything in Aunt Tab's house was sticky. The walls and the door knobs. The mirror where they stared at their chopped-off hair. The

sheets and pillows of their small chilly beds. It was as if sticky fingers had rubbed or touched or prodded every last thing.

"Tom," Ellie whispered in bed that night, "do you think we will be all right?"

"Of course we will," Tom said. "Just a bit sticky."

Chapter 3
The Treacle Pond

The first night at Aunt Tab's would have been awful without Whiskers. Tom and Ellie did not sleep well. First one, and then the other woke up and stared sadly into the dark.

Whiskers seemed to know how lonely they felt. She jumped onto their beds, warm and purring and not even a little bit sticky. Ever since she arrived at Aunt Tab's she had been washing herself. She was a clean cat, as well as kind.

“I don’t see how Aunt Tab can’t like her,” Ellie said.

But Aunt Tab didn’t like her. Not a bit.

“I’ve never seen such horrid fluff,” she said when she poked her head round Ellie’s bedroom door the next morning. “And I hope none of those awful whiskers are loose! If they are they will have to go! *Snip, snap!* Now, children, a lovely breakfast is waiting in the kitchen ... Cornflakes. Eggs ... and treacle."

Ellie opened her mouth to protest, and then she remembered not to fuss and closed it again.

"And then school ..." Aunt Tab went on. "And after school a nice trip to the beach to see if anything's washed up from your parents' raft ... Did you groan, Tom dear?"

"No, I growled," Tom said.

"No growling please," said Aunt Tab and she smiled at him with her head on one side. "As I was saying, beach. Then homework. Then supper. Then bed."

"Let's run away," Ellie said, when she and Tom were alone. "How can I go to school with hair like this? And who will look after Whiskers while we are out? And I don't WANT to look for bits of raft on the beach! What if we find some?"

"We won't find any because they DIDN'T SINK," Tom said. "And Whiskers will be OK. She's a clever cat. Your hair looks quite nice, a bit like a bonfire. And we can't run away because we have nowhere to run to."

Ellie said nothing. She felt too gloomy.

Tom read the list of rules.

"What pond?" he asked and he pointed to **Rule Number 4 – NO PLAYING IN THE PRIVATE POND!**

"What pond? Where is it? And why is it private?"

"Perhaps we'll find out at school," Ellie said. "That is, if anyone talks to us."

"Of course they will!"

"We'll be New," Ellie said. "Perhaps they won't."

Ellie need not have worried. Loads of people talked to them. Everyone had heard about the raft. Everyone knew where they were living.

And Whiskers came to school with them and everyone thought she was beautiful.

"You call the woman you live with Aunt Tab," the other children said, "but we call her the Sticky Witch! The pond is her treacle pond. Have you seen it yet?"

"No," Tom and Ellie said.

"Well, you will," someone said. "She's always cleaning it out. She can't bear fluff in it. It blocks up the treacle fountain pump. The fountain's on a little island right in the middle of the pond and the treacle bubbles out."

"But what does Aunt Tab do with a treacle pond?" Ellie asked.

"Oh, the normal things," the boy said. "Toads, mostly."

"Show us your treacle pond!" Ellie begged Aunt Tab when she rushed home that night.

"I thought you were going to go to the beach, dear," said Aunt Tab. "To see what is left of your parents' raft."

"There's nothing left," Ellie said.

"Fancy that, sunk without trace!" Aunt Tab said. "And how do you know about my treacle pond?"

"They told us at school!"

Aunt Tab smiled a terrible sticky, witchy smile. "If I show you my pond will you promise not to paddle?" she said.

"Oh, yes!" both Tom and Ellie said.

"And promise never to stir, lick, drink or dabble?"

"Yes, yes!" they said.

"And never let that cat go diving?" Aunt Tab said.

"Never, never," Ellie promised.

"Very well then," Aunt Tab said, and she led the way.

The pond was as round as a ring, with a flat, smooth edge of white stone. It glowed with a sticky golden light.

"Is it very deep?" Tom asked.

"Very deep," said Aunt Tab. "But there's a plug in the middle. You reach it from the island. Do you see my pet?"

Tom and Ellie looked. In the middle of the pond was a small stone island in the shape of a water lily. From the middle of the island a very slow fountain ran with golden treacle. At the very edge of the island, as far as he could get from the fountain, sat a toad.

"How did he get there?" Ellie asked.

"I put him there," Aunt Tab said. "Long, long ago."

The pond was beautiful. And it was awful.

"You may dip in one finger," Aunt Tab said. "And have one suck."

"No thank you," they said, with a shudder.

"It is my great treasure," said Aunt Tab.

Tom and Ellie wrote a postcard. It said –

Dear Parents

Did you know there are 365 days in a year?
You said that you'd be back in 3 years.
That is 1,095 days.
And 1,095 nights.
So far we have done 2 days.
And 1 night.

Love from Tom and Ellie and Whiskers the Cat.

They put it in another bottle and threw it out to sea.

"It isn't fussing, is it?" Ellie asked, as she watched the message bob away on the waves.

"No," said Tom. "It's maths."

Chapter 4
The Toad

Days at Aunt Tab's began to fall into a pattern. School. Beach. Home. Bed. In between everything was treacle. Treacle meals. Treacle smells. Treacle stickiness.

Tom and Ellie got used to school and beach and home and bed but they never got used to the stickiness.

Sticky zips and cuffs and buttons took a long time every morning. Sticky stairs, sticky

curtains and sticky slippers slowed everything down at the end of the day.

Sticky homework took hours. The pencils stuck to their fingers and books had to be peeled from the table. It was worst of all when Aunt Tab came to watch.

"May I see?" she would ask, and she would reach out a sticky arm and turn over the pages of their books with sticky fingers. "Very well done!" she would say, and she would pat their heads and leave sticky tangles in their hair.

Ellie tried to make herself not mind.

"It doesn't hurt," she said one day. "It doesn't sting. It doesn't tickle. It doesn't itch. It shouldn't be awful."

"It is awful," Tom said. "It's the worst thing in the world."

Ellie said the worst thing in the world was the way their parents' raft had vanished between one green wave and another.

Tom would not agree.

"We go to the beach every day," he said, "and we never find any bits of raft. Any day now we will hear from them. You'll see."

This day, more than ever, Tom wished that he and Ellie could run away.

At school that lunch-time they had heard a new story about Aunt Tab. A boy called Peter told them.

"It was last year," Peter said, "before you came. I was just outside the Sticky Witch's garden, behind the hedge. I was trying to see the treacle pond."

"Did you see it?" Tom asked.

“Yes,” Peter said. “I’d never seen it before and I thought it was amazing. It was much bigger than I thought it would be ... And have you seen the bit in the middle, the island in the shape of a water lily?”

“Yes,” said Ellie.

“Well, two toads were sitting there. Right at the edge. One yellow, and one green. And the yellow toad said to the green toad ...”

“What?” Tom and Ellie shouted. “Toads can’t talk!”

Peter ignored them and went on ... “The yellow toad said to the green toad, ‘How did you get here? Did you swim?’

“‘Swim?’ the green toad said. ‘I was chucked, that’s how I got here. Chucked, in the middle of the night.’

"'Same as me then,' the yellow toad said. 'What does she want us here for, anyway?'

"'Thinks we'll grant her wishes,' the green toad said. 'Some toads can.'"

Tom and Ellie's mouths hung open in shock, but Whiskers didn't look surprised at all. Perhaps she'd always known that some toads can talk, and a few can even grant wishes. She was a very clever cat.

"'Well, I can't do wishes,' the yellow toad said, 'and I'm not waiting here till that witch finds out. I'm going to swim for it!'

"And then," Peter went on, "I saw the yellow toad slide into the treacle and start to swim. He'd just got going when she came along. The Sticky Witch. She came down the garden path to the pond, smiling and singing ..."

"Oh," Ellie groaned, and Tom said, "I hate it when she sings."

"I wanted to run away," Peter said. "I was scared, all of a sudden. I don't know why. But that toad was still swimming, and the other one was doing something very odd. He was hopping very fast from one side of the island to the other."

"He was trying to look like two toads," Tom guessed, and Peter nodded.

"The other one was having an awful time. It was so hard to swim in that treacle," Peter went on. "Only his nose showed – like a tiny dark arrow. I thought the Sticky Witch hadn't seen him. She just kept smiling and humming and I kept watching until at last the yellow toad made it right across the pond to the other side. And then he began to climb up the rim ..."

"Thank goodness," Ellie whispered.

"The treacle poured off him and ran back into the pond," Peter said. "And his sides went in and out as if he was panting and the green

toad hopped faster and faster and the Sticky Witch smiled and hummed and she said, 'Silly.'"

"Silly?" Ellie said.

"Yes," Peter said. "And she poked him back into the pond with the toe of her shoe ... and he sank. The green toad in the middle went very still. But she was still smiling and humming. And then I must have made a sound ..."

"What sort of a sound?" Ellie asked.

"A scream, or something," Peter said. "Because she saw me. The Sticky Witch came over to the hedge and she bent and peered at me and she laughed and she said, 'Silly!'"

"Then what?" Tom asked.

"Then I ran," said Peter.

Whiskers chose the postcard they bought after school that day. It was a picture of a toad on a lily leaf. Whiskers would not let them write on it. She carried it home in her teeth.

Chapter 5
In the Middle of the Night

As Tom and Ellie walked back to Aunt Tab's, they talked about Peter's terrible story.

"Perhaps," Ellie said, "perhaps she thought she was being kind. Putting that yellow toad back into the pond. Perhaps she didn't know he would sink."

"Are you mad?" Tom asked.

"No," Ellie said. "It just makes her a bit less scary to think of her like that."

"Aunt Tab," Tom said in a bossy voice, "is sticky! Not scary!"

Ellie didn't reply.

"I hope you're not turning into a scaredy cat," said Tom.

"I hope you're not turning into bossy pig," said Ellie.

It was the first time they'd had a quarrel.

They walked home in a sulk. They ate treacle pancakes in a sulk and then went to bed, still in a sulk. Whiskers didn't like bad tempers. She didn't come and sit on their beds and purr. At bedtime she propped her postcard up at the top of the stairs and sat beside it and glared at them.

It was hours before either of them guessed what she wanted them to do.

When Ellie guessed she shivered.

When Tom guessed his heart thumped hard and fast.

Ellie got up. She thought Tom was asleep. She got out of bed and tiptoed down to the treacle pond.

Tom got up too. He thought Ellie was asleep. He got out of bed and tiptoed down to the treacle pond.

They arrived at the pond the same moment.

"What are you doing here?" Tom asked, when he saw Ellie.

"I'm rescuing the toad," Ellie said. "What are you doing here?"

"I'm rescuing the toad," said Tom. "Where do you think Whiskers is?"

"Outside Aunt Tab's bedroom door," Ellie said.

"She's keeping guard," Tom guessed.

They both felt a bit better at the thought of Whiskers keeping guard.

"Still, we'd better hurry," Ellie said, and they both turned to look at the pond.

Silver moonlight shone on the dark gold pond. They could see the toad, a lumpy shape in the middle. He looked a long way away.

"I think I might be able to jump it," Tom said. "But if I do I expect you'll say I'm being a bossy pig."

"A boat would be good," Ellie said, "but I think I might be able to swim it. And if I don't I expect you'll say I'm a scaredy cat so ..."

"NO!" Tom shouted, but Ellie was already in the treacle.

Ellie was stuck fast in the treacle like a spoon in honey. Like a fly trapped in a cobweb. The treacle came up to her neck.

Then up to her chin.

Then up to her nose.

Ellie was choking in the treacle!

Tom was too far behind to help. The lily leaf island was too far in front to reach. Ellie was sinking.

"Hang on!" Tom called, and he jumped.

What a jump! From the rim of the pond to the lily leaf island! Tom was still too far away, but something had changed. Ellie wasn't sinking any more. She was spinning. A slow

spin, then faster, round and round the lily leaf island.

Tom had pulled out the plug and Ellie was gurgling towards the plug hole in a whirlpool of treacle.

Just in time, Ellie caught the stone edge of the lily leaf island.

First with her fingers.

Then with her hands.

And then she was out of the treacle and sitting on the lily leaf.

With Tom.

And the toad.

All three of them were covered in treacle.

“I couldn’t jump back,” Tom said.

"I couldn't swim back," Ellie said.

All around them, pale silver and dark gold, the treacle drained away.

"I had to pull the plug out," Tom said. "It was the only way I could think of to stop you sinking."

"Thank you," Ellie said. "It was a great jump."

"It was a brave swim," said Tom.

The pond became a dark, steep pit, with sticky sides. They didn't feel at all safe on the lily leaf fountain with its thin lily leaf stalk.

The last of the treacle glugged down the plug hole and the treacle fountain stopped.

"We'll just have to wait," said Ellie.

Chapter 6
Whiskers

Something moved on the far side of the pond.

A rustle.

And the sound of scrabbling feet.

It was Whiskers, the cleverest cat in the world. And she was dragging a hose pipe in her teeth.

When she got to the rim of the pond, an arch of silver shot in the air.

Water, the only thing in the world that could save them.

It poured over Tom and Ellie. It poured over the toad.

All the stickiness was washed away.

And then they put the plug back in the treacle pond.

"The pond will fill with water," they told the toad, "and we'll be able to swim across."

"And then I'll grant you three wishes," said the toad.

Tom and Ellie were so surprised that they nearly fell off the lily leaf. Peter had told them that the toad could speak, but somehow they hadn't expected it to happen. After all, he looked a very normal sort of toad.

"Wishes?" Tom asked. "Can you really grant wishes for people?"

"I can," the toad said. "As long as you rescue me first."

"Then why didn't you wish yourself away from the treacle pond?" Ellie asked.

"I can grant wishes for other people," the toad said. "Not for myself! Good grief, there wouldn't be a genie left in a bottle anywhere if magic creatures could grant wishes for themselves!"

"How unfair!" Ellie said.

"Not at all," said the toad. "It's the first rule of magic. And since I can grant wishes for other people, you get three. One each, and one for the cat. I do think you might say ..."

"Thank you!" Tom and Ellie said together. "Oh, thank you! But ..."

"Don't say 'but'," the toad said. "Get thinking, before the pond fills up and I swim away!"

Tom and Ellie had always had a plan in case they were given a wish. The plan was to wish that all the other wishes they wanted would come true. That way they could turn one wish into hundreds.

"Cheating," the toad said when he heard this plan. "Think again."

Tom thought of wishing they were off the lily leaf and safe on the other side. But that was a waste of a wish, because all they had to do was wait until the water was deep enough to swim.

Ellie thought of wishing that their parents' raft hadn't sunk and that it never would. But Tom said the raft hadn't sank and it wouldn't. So that would be a waste of a wish too.

"Yesterday," Ellie said, "we'd have wished for no more treacle."

"There is no more treacle," said Tom. "There's only a few splashes left. It's a waste to wish away a few splashes of treacle. It's getting light. Had you noticed?"

"I noticed the moon had gone," said Ellie.

"Morning is coming. It always comes in a rush when it starts," said Tom.

It did come in a rush. One bird sang and then a tree full of birds. The sky turned pink.

"Very pretty," the toad said. "Now hurry up with those wishes!"

"I wouldn't mind being very pretty," Ellie said.

"You look OK as you are," Tom said kindly. "I wouldn't mind being fantastic at something. Like flying or football."

"You're already fantastic at jumping," Ellie said. "One fantastic is enough. Any more would be showing off. When shall we start swimming? Is it deep enough yet?"

"Soon," said Tom.

"Very soon," the toad agreed. "So get on with those wishes!"

Tom and Ellie began to make a list of things worth wishing for.

Money – and lots of it.

Time travel.

World peace.

The power to talk to animals.

And their own castle with a real moat and drawbridge.

All the time that they were talking, Whiskers was filling the treacle pond.

"Whiskers, Whiskers!" Ellie called. "Did you know you had a wish?"

Whiskers looked back at Ellie.

"Do you think she understands?" Ellie asked.

"Of course," said Tom. "She's the cleverest cat in the world. When will the wishes come true?"

"When you rescue me," the toad said, and as he spoke the water lapped over the rim of the lily leaf.

The toad gave a great sigh of relief, slipped into the pond and began to swim.

He was across in a moment.

Then over the rim.

And then he vanished into the shadows.

"We rescued him," Ellie said. "Lovely! But how I wish the yellow toad had been saved too."

"Ellie!" Tom groaned.

"What?" Ellie asked.

Just then two happy croaks came from the bushes. "Nothing," Tom said. "Tell you later. Our turn now."

"Yes," Ellie agreed. "Come on!"

She jumped into the water and started to swim.

It was a moment before Tom followed. He was not such a good swimmer as Ellie, and he had a feeling that the water in the treacle pond was as cold as ice.

"Oh," he gasped, as he slid in. "I wish it was a bit warmer."

In an instant, it became a bit warmer.

"Tom!" Ellie wailed. "Your wish is gone!"

"Well, so is yours," said Tom.

"Mine? How?"

"The yellow toad! Didn't you hear? That was your wish!" Tom said.

"Oh!" Ellie gasped. "Oh, yes, of course."

"We'll just have to do without wishes," said Tom.

It was not a good time to do without wishes. As Ellie and Tom splashed and wished and gasped, a dark shape ran down the garden path.

There was no one to help poor Whiskers! A moment later, the Sticky Witch grabbed her.

"How many times do I have to tell you?" she screeched. "NO FLUFF NEAR THE TREACLE POND!"

She swooped Whiskers high in the air with a large sticky hand.

For a second, all the birds stopped singing.

In that second, the Sticky Witch saw that the pond was not golden any more. It was a bright, lovely blue, the colour of the sky.

And she saw that the only things in the pond were two dripping wet children.

Her toad was gone, and all his wishes with him.

Then the Sticky Witch screeched and hurled Whiskers high into the air.

Whiskers yowled.

Ellie and Tom wailed.

And then everything changed, because Whiskers had a wish to make too.

As she shot through the sky, this is what Whiskers wished. "I wish that toad would do something to help."

And he did.

By the time Tom and Ellie were safe on the ground, the magic had worked.

Aunt Tab was a cat.

And Whiskers was Aunt Tab.

After that there was nothing left to do except live happily ever after.

Chapter 7
Ever After

Aunt Tab was not a friendly cat. She was thin and bad-tempered and she spat. She only settled down a bit when Ellie had the good idea of giving her a saucer of treacle. It looked a bit like her pond.

After that, every day, she sat by her saucer and growled if anyone came near. Then a circus came to the village and stole Aunt Tab. Ellie, Tom and Whiskers didn't miss her one bit.

Aunt Tab became very famous as the World's Stickiest Cat.

The treacle pond became a wildlife pond, full of happy toads. They didn't grant wishes. This didn't matter, because Tom and Ellie had nothing left to wish for. The same day that the wishes came true the postman arrived with a postcard which he'd found on the beach washed up in a bottle. It said –

Not sunk yet.
Thanks for all the postcards!
Much love from Mum and Dad on the raft!

So that was all right.

Whiskers was a perfect aunt. She was merry, fluffy and interested in everything. She never gave Tom or Ellie food made with treacle.

In fact, she never made any food at all. Tom and Ellie soon became very good at cooking.

Even as an aunt, Whiskers had lovely soft whiskers and a swishing striped tail. Sometimes she washed her ears with her paws. Often she purred when the sun shone.

Sometimes she hardly seemed like a person at all.

Much more like a golden tiger-sized tabby cat.

The next three years went in a flash. All the postcards that Tom and Ellie sent were happy.

Having a lovely time.

So don't hurry back!

With love from Tom and Ellie and Whiskers the Cat.

Our books are tested
for children and young people by
children and young people.

Thanks to everyone who consulted on
a manuscript for their time and effort in
helping us to make our books better
for our readers.